The Kingdom of Summerdale Street

Written by Quentin Flynn
Illustrated by Ian Forss

Contents

NELSON
CENGAGE Learning
For learning solutions, visit cengage.com.au

Meet the Characters

King Clive I

Otherwise known as Dad.

Queen Stephanie

Otherwise known as Mum.

Princess Melanie

Otherwise known as the narrator.

A Scoundrel

Otherwise known as a council watering inspector.

A Fine Legal Mind

Otherwise known as a lawyer at Loopholes-R-Us.

A Royal Hound

Otherwise known as Valiant.

Dear Reader

I've often thought it would be a good idea to be a king. I'm sure I'd be a very popular ruler, because there'd be lots of new laws outlawing broccoli and making jam doughnuts compulsory for breakfast. I hope you enjoy this story about someone else who decides to be a king – and maybe it'll give you some ideas for your own kingdom!

Quentin Flynn
Author

The Kingdom of Summerdale Street

1. The palace
2. The royal roses
3. The royal limousine
4. The site of the Battle of Bratwurst
5. The ambassador's residence
6. Foreign lands

The Opening Chapter

In which the remarkable crowning of the most nobell monarch of this excellent kingdom is well descrybed with much accuracy and meticulous attention to detayle as witnessed by jubilant spectators gathered thereat for this illustrious moment.

"The much anticipated coronation of His Most Glorious Majesty, King Clive I, Defender of Liberty, Sovereign of Summerdale and Guardian of the Imperial Trident, was a thoroughly magnificent affair, where the supreme grandeur of His Majesty outshone even the glittering splendour of the priceless crown jewels.

Following the triumphant ceremony, which was attended by privileged royalty, distinguished ambassadors, glamorous celebrities and representatives of the world's media, a sumptuous state banquet ensued, and rejoicing to mark this auspicious event continued long into the evening."

A Humble and Fully Verified Eyewitness Account of the Ushering In of the Clivarian Era of Prosperity and Graciousness (Vol. I)

There are, of course, always two versions of history: the officially sanctioned version of events and the true story. King Clive I (or "Dad", as I call him) appointed Queen Stephanie (or "Mum", as she's known informally around here) to write *A Humble and Fully Verified Eyewitness Account of the Ushering in of the Clivarian Era of Prosperity and Graciousness.* After he had scoured the thesaurus for words like "glorious", "magnificent", "grandeur", 'distinguished" and "splendour", and made her add these to her first draft, this became the official version, part of which you've just read.

Here's what really happened. The unofficial, unauthorised version.

Dad went down to the local $2 shop and found a toy plastic crown that was missing its price tag (so it was, I admit, priceless). Mum was the "privileged royalty", our neighbour, Mrs Willis, was the "distinguished ambassador", Aunty Thea (who had once had her photo mistakenly broadcast on Crimewatch) was a "glamorous celebrity" and a bemused Korean tourist with a camera represented the world's media.

After the ceremony, which involved Mum flinging the crown up in the air and Dad catching it on his head like

a dog catching a frisbee, Dad cooked us all a barbecue (using his imperial trident, or “barbecue fork” as we like to call it). Then we watched a wildlife program on TV about the secret life of snails until Aunty Thea’s snoring got too loud, and we all decided to call it a night. The Korean tourist looked quite relieved.

Out of the two versions, I know which one will probably end up, stamped with gilded coats of arms and bound in the finest leather, in the repository of the Royal Clivarian Palace Library (otherwise known as the bookshelf).

I suppose I should really get into the spirit of things because I am, after all, apparently a princess now. Princess Melanie of Summerdale. And one day, when the burdens of being a majesty, a defender, a sovereign and a guardian get too much for Dad, he’ll abdicate and make me Queen Mel. When that happens, I’ll probably think that the official history of our kingdom isn’t so bad after all. Kings and queens rarely seem to disagree with florid descriptions of their glorious magnificence, and I don’t suppose I’ll be any different.

But until then, here’s my unofficial history of how it all really came about.

II The Subsequent Chapter

In which are set forth, wyth excellent penmanship, the consyquences of a sojourn amongst the meadows of this fayre land, where the pitiless tyranny and shameful injustices which runneth rampant 'neath her dry and dusky heavens are revealed.

"The bravery of the feisty and overwhelmingly handsome nobleman, whose destiny it was to become ruler of all the lands which make up the Kingdom of Summerdale, lay undiscovered and unappreciated until, one evening, fate disclosed its hand. Henceforth, this day has been celebrated annually with a festive holiday, known as Rainwater Tuesday.

Rose petals are traditionally scattered on driveways and footpaths as a reminder of the deeds that first set King Clive I upon his path to glory."

A Humble and Fully Verified Eyewitness Account of the Ushering In of the Clivarian Era of Prosperity and Graciousness (Vol. II)

The Kingdom of Summerdale had its humble beginnings on a Tuesday; that much is true. Tuesdays, as everyone in Summerdale Street

should have known, were no-watering days, when you weren't allowed to use a hose to water your garden.

After a couple of weeks with no rain, however, Dad decided he'd sneak out after dark and give his prized roses a much-needed drink. The entire history of the Kingdom of Summerdale might have been changed forever if he'd remembered to do it on Monday (when watering was allowed) but, as is often the case, history is shaped by small, seemingly insignificant events. I was inside finishing my homework and Mum was on the computer. And Dad was outside.

With a flick of his wrist, the tap was turned, and with it, so too was the course of our lives.

"Oi!" came a voice from the darkness. "You can't do that!"

"It's alright," explained Dad to the mysterious figure wagging its finger at him from the other side of the street. "It's rainwater. It comes off the roof and into the rainwater tank."

"Have you got an exemption permit?" asked the figure. "You need an RWE315."

"A what?" said Dad, sounding perplexed.

"An RWE315," sighed the figure, as if everyone knew what an RWE315 was. "It's an exemption from watering restrictions issued by the council in cases where rainwater tanks are used to water gardens instead of the town water supply."

"Well, I am using rainwater," repeated Dad. "Anyway, who are you?"

"I'm a council watering inspector, duly authorised by council directive 29F to check whether RWE315s have been issued in accordance with town planning ordinance 604C."

The figure walked up the driveway, past Mum's car, and Dad saw that he was indeed wearing an orange vest emblazoned with the words "Council Watering Inspector".

"So have you got an RWE315?" repeated the inspector.

"No," said Dad. "But you're welcome to check where the hose is connected, because the rainwater tank is just over there."

"Can't do that," said the inspector bluntly, shaking his head. "Inspections of water sources require an IWS55 to be submitted to a council plumbing inspector duly authorised by council directive 809B." He tapped the words on his orange vest. "I'm a watering inspector, not a plumbing inspector."

COUNCIL
WATERING
INSPECTOR

Dad shook his head in exasperation, and the watering inspector pulled a thick booklet of forms from his pocket.

"I'm issuing you with an infringement notice," he declared, clicking a ballpoint pen into action. "Watering on a non-watering day and failure to supply on request an RWE315 showing that rainwater is being used."

"But it is being used!" protested Dad. Forgetting he had a hose in one hand, he turned around in agitation and accidentally sprinkled water over the inspector's trousers.

The inspector looked down at his trousers and slowly shook his head. "Grievous interference with a duly authorised inspector attempting to carry out his duties," he sighed wearily. "We get troublemakers like you all the time," he added.

"It's just water!" said Dad. "*RAIN*WATER!"

The council inspector ignored Dad, finished writing up his infringement notices and handed Dad a handful of pink slips. Dad's mouth fell when he added up what was written at the bottom of the slips.

"$350!" he said in disbelief.

“Have a nice evening, sir,” said the watering inspector as he walked back down the driveway. “And turn that hose off.”

That’s when Dad copped another fine, this time for $750. Who would have ever thought that deliberately hosing down a council inspector at full pressure was such an expensive exercise? Twice as expensive, as it happens, on a non-watering day.

III The Myddle Chapter

In which an examination is made of how tyranny was overthrown and hence discarded by the lionhart, Clive, at his magnanimous victory agaynst fearsome oddes at the struggle henceforth known to all as the Battle of Bratwurst.

Dad was indignant enough after receiving council fines totalling $1100. But when he emptied the letterbox the next morning and found a council notice declaring that all residents' cars would, from next month, be required to display a resident parking sticker (available for an annual charge of $12), he was furious.

Dad stormed into the kitchen, where Mum and I were having breakfast. "They're charging me to park my own car in my own street outside my own house!" he spluttered. "That's ridiculous."

"There's plenty of room up the driveway, Dad,"

I pointed out between mouthfuls of cereal. "You can just park up behind Mum's car."

Dad shook his head. "It's the principle," he replied obstinately. "It's about the erosion of freedom in our society, the death of democracy and the removal of our rights as human beings."

"It's a parking sticker," said Mum, who was waiting for her toast to pop up from the toaster.

"No, no," said Dad. "It's the thin end of the wedge, because first they'll charge us for parking our cars, then they'll charge us for walking along pavements, and where will it all stop? Next they'll charge us for just living here!"

"They already do, dear," said Mum patiently. "They're called rates."

Dad rattled the council letter brusquely. "Hmm," he said, which he felt was always a cleverly decisive way to win discussions, especially with Mum.

"Besides, they're the council and there's absolutely nothing we can do about it," finished Mum. Her toast popped up.

"Hmm," said Dad again. He pulled the wrapper off the morning newspaper. Then he got really irritated.

"Pah!" he snorted. "'Due to the recent dry weather a limited fire ban is being imposed by the city council,'" he read. "'BB99 permits will be required for all open fires, including barbecues. Residents who wish to apply for a BB99 should call the council on the number below.'"

Dad looked at Mum, as if he was inviting her to share his horror at such an authoritarian and thoroughly unjustified infringement of his rights to start a wildfire and burn down our house. She just buttered her toast.

"It has been rather dry," she observed.

"But not dry enough to actually impose a real fire ban," puffed Dad. "A piece of paper issued by some bureaucrat at the council means you can incinerate to your heart's content. That's not fair. If it's safe enough to burn sausages on my barbecue with a piece of paper, it's safe enough to burn them without a piece of paper. I'm perfectly capable of deciding whether to do it or not – not some council ninny!"

"OK, dear," said Mum.

"In fact, I'm feeling like sausages tonight," said Dad defiantly. "Nice, chargrilled sausages. That's decided then. We're having a barbecue. One without paper."

"Hmm," said Mum.

If Dad had listened to the tone of Mum's "hmm", he might have wisely decided not to have a barbecue. But he didn't, and that was another turning point for the Kingdom of Summerdale. Instead, he headed next door to invite Mrs Willis, our neighbour, over for dinner.

"In the annals of history, the 'Glorious Defeat of the Forces of the Enemy at the Battle of Bratwurst' will forever be remembered as a decisive moment for the fledgling monarchy of Summerdale. As with most legends shrouded in the mists of time, the chivalrous feats of the courageous heroes will grow in bravery each time the legend is retold."

A Humble and Fully Verified Eyewitness Account of the Ushering In of the Clivarian Era of Prosperity and Graciousness (Vol. III)

Actually, it wasn't so much the "mists of time" as the smoke from Dad's barbecue.

"Children will recreate the parry and thrust of the opposing forces as they re-enact the battle in playgrounds around the world.

Authors and filmmakers will depict the epic struggle in bestsellers and blockbusters, and jolly minstrels will sing of the dangers and heroism witnessed in the heat of battle.

Generations from now, scholars of Clivarian history will still talk about the gallantry that the Battle of Bratwurst inspired. Some details will be discussed, over and over again, some will grow with time, and some will be lost."

A Humble and Fully Verified Eyewitness Account of the Ushering In of the Clivarian Era of Prosperity and Graciousness (Vol. III)

Like the fact that it was all over a sausage.

Looking back, I suspect Dad didn't even clean the barbecue, in order to make it smokier than usual. And, even though he only had half-a-dozen bratwurst sausages to cook, he turned up all six burners on his barbecue to "full". As a result, a mushroom cloud of freshly incinerated lamb chop grease and kebab fragments from our previous barbecue drifted defiantly into the air.

Our dog, Valiant, turned up shortly after the scent of charred food particles filled the backyard. He sat patiently, eyeing Dad's every gesture, waiting for a morsel to fly off his wildly waving barbecue fork.

Mrs Willis turned up a few minutes after the smoke wafted across the fence and into her backyard, and sat in a deckchair, doing her knitting.

And then the malevolent forces of the arch-enemy turned up, in the guise of a clean air inspector from ... you guessed it, the city council.

"Hello, sir," he said to Dad cheerily. "It's a popular night for a barbecue. I've checked four in this suburb alone this evening."

"Checked them for what?" bristled Dad, concentrating on the delicate task of bratwurst turning.

"Permits, sir," replied the inspector. The poor man still didn't suspect a thing. "We're just checking everyone's got a BB99. It's a health and safety issue, sir."

Dad whirled around, sensing a looming philosophical checkmate.

"So, if I have a BB99, my barbecue is healthy and safe," he said, sounding thoughtful. "But if I don't have a BB99, it's unhealthy and dangerous." He raised an eyebrow perilously at the hapless inspector.

"Well, no, sir," said the man uncomfortably. "But the rules state you must have a permit to operate your barbecue."

INSPECTOR

"AHA!" crowed Dad, pointing his barbecue fork accusingly at the inspector, who took a nervous step back. "That's OK then. I do have a permit." He grinned, reached into his back pocket and handed a folded piece of paper to the clean air inspector.

"What's this?" said the inspector in a puzzled voice.

"A CP1," sighed Dad, as if everyone knew what a CP1 was. "It's a permit to set anything I like on fire, especially bratwursts. A Clive Permit 1."

"Is it issued by the council?" said the inspector, peering at the handwritten note.

"No," said Dad airily, "it's issued with full authority by me."

"But ... you can't just issue your own permits, sir," said the inspector hesitantly.

"Why not?" smiled Dad triumphantly.

"Well, er ..." The council inspector was nonplussed. "Look, sir, I'm not going to argue with you. If you don't turn off your barbecue, I'll have to turn it off myself and issue you with an infringement notice."

A steely glint came into Dad's eyes. The gauntlet had been thrown down. He whirled around, picked up a sausage and defiantly chomped off the top half.

"Pofeckly healfy," he said, baring his teeth ever so slightly (mainly because the sausage was so hot it burned his tongue). "Pofeckly saff."

Finally, he couldn't bear it any longer and spat out the white-hot lump of bratwurst. It hit the clean air inspector smack-bang in the middle of his forehead.

The forces of the enemy at the Battle of Bratwurst were thus gloriously defeated, in the first documented instance of a bratwurst being used as a weapon. Unfortunately, that didn't stop the council issuing Dad with another fine for grievous interference with a duly authorised inspector attempting to carry out his duties.

And, as he subsequently discovered, assault with a sausage was three times as expensive as a thorough hosing with rainwater.

IV The Consequent Chapter

In which the discerning reader may enjoy the tale of how the sovereign castles and meadows of Summerdale become freed from the yoke of unfayre burdens imposed thereon by wycked foreign powers and the liberties of a new kyngdom are bestowed forthwith upon its inhabytants.

Facing fines totalling $3350 and a court order forbidding him to come within ten metres of a council employee if he was carrying cooked delicatessen items, Dad finally decided it was time to find himself a lawyer.

Instead of meticulously consulting dusty volumes of constitutional law, the lawyer at Loopholes-R-Us spent most of her consultation time with Dad kicking the photocopy machine.

"You can't win against the council," she said, opening a side door and peering into the machine's innards.

"Why not?" said Dad.

The lawyer jiggled some toner bottles deep within the photocopier. "Look, as long as you live in this country, you have to obey the laws of this country,

and one of the laws you're expected to adhere to prohibits the endangerment of council employees through the wilful misuse of sausages."

"So, as long as I live here, the council has the right to interfere with my life as much as it wants," said Dad.

The lawyer shrugged her shoulders. "That's pretty much it," she said. She pressed the copy button on the machine and a half a sheet of paper whirred through the roller before jamming with an infuriating whine and crumple.

"Hmm," said Dad. The Kingdom of Summerdale was mere moments away. "What if I didn't live here?" he said. "What if I lived in a different country?"

"Well, you'd have to obey the laws of that country, too," said the lawyer in an exasperated tone. "And I daresay most countries look very dimly on assault with a sausage." She slapped the side of the machine fruitlessly.

"Not if it was my own country!" said Dad. "Not if I declared independence and set up my own country. What's to stop me doing that? The council would have no authority whatsoever in my country."

The lawyer pulled out the jammed sheet of paper. "Good luck with that," she said, opening another drawer on the photocopier and searching for a new ream of paper.

"I have the blessing of the finest legal minds in the country," Dad reassured Mum. "They said 'good luck', and you can't get more definitive than that."

"But you can't just start your own country, Dad," I said.

"People do it all the time," said Dad. "People in other countries."

"So how exactly does it work, dear?" asked Mum mischievously. "You'll probably have to fill in a form. Shall I go onto the council website and see if I can find the one for declaring independence?"

"Ha, ha," said Dad. "I know you think I'm being silly, but look at all the countries that were already part of another country when they decided to declare independence. The United States, for example. I bet they didn't fill out a form and email it to King George III."

"Dad's right there," I pointed out. It wasn't often I said that to Mum. She rolled her eyes.

Meanwhile, I could see that Dad was deep in thought.

"King George III," he said to himself. "That's given me an idea. Why not King Clive I? I shall declare independence and proclaim myself King Clive I of Summerdale. That'll give the council something to ponder."

"Well, at least King Clive I and King George III will have something in common," said Mum.

"Really?" said Dad, delighted at Mum's support for his forthcoming regal status.

"Yes," said Mum. "He was mad and you are too."

Once Dad had an idea in his head, there was little anyone could do to stop him. I have to admit his research was meticulous. He went on the internet and searched for "constitutional precedents for not being allowed to establish your own kingdom in Summerdale Street."

"No results found," said the search page.

"Almost 8 billion pages on the web," crowed Dad triumphantly. "And not one sound legal reason why I can't set up my own kingdom."

And that was that. The combined resources of the internet and Loopholes-R-Us couldn't be wrong, so Dad hurried off to find a piece of paper.

"Are you sure you want to do this?" queried the woman at the advertising desk at the local paper. She reread the piece of paper that Dad had handed over.

"Great troubles require great leaders," replied Dad.

"I'll need a proper address," said the woman. "For the bill."

Dad looked at what he had written at the bottom of the paper. *King Clive, The Palace, Kingdom of Summerdale.*

"That is a proper address, madam," replied Dad. "But if you like, I'll pay by credit card now. Just in case."

"I think that would be a good idea," said the woman.

And so King Clive I's declaration of independence was published in the local paper, between advertisements for Butcher Bob's Weekly Special (prime mince, only

$5.99 a kilo) and Magical Meg's Clairvoyant Predictions (call now, only $1.99 a minute for astrological secrets revealed). The Kingdom of Summerdale was officially launched. And we had Butcher Bob's mince for tea, because Dad declared he wanted to foster international trading relationships.

"In an inspiring and powerful summary of the inalienable rights of its subjects, the Summerdale Declaration of Independence was proclaimed on Thursday, 17 May:

We, the people of 5A Summerdale Street solemnly publish and declare that all who live behind our front garden fence are, from this day forth, grateful subjects of a free and independent state, henceforth known as the Kingdom of Summerdale. As such, we have full power to water gardens, park our cars, operate barbecues, and do all other acts and things which independent states may of right do. We also declare that our ruler shall be the splendid King Clive I, who shall exercise his regal rights and powers (along with his dog, Valiant) with grace and fairness and for the good of all the peoples of this fair nation."

A Humble and Fully Verified Eyewitness Account of the Ushering In of the Clivarian Era of Prosperity and Graciousness (Vol. IV)

In the original draft (now held under tight security in the Clivarian Palace Library), the wording of the last sentence had been slightly different, but Mum had refused to allow Dad the regal rights and powers to not mow the lawns or do the dishes. As Mum pointed out, the famous document called Magna Carta, which was created by the feudal barons of England and formed the basis of our modern legal system, forced King John to relinquish some of his powers. Dad wisely decided to back down. He figured that kings and queens still got to do pretty much what they wanted anyway, and if the people of Summerdale revolted against his benevolent reign later, he'd just incarcerate them in a dungeon.

"Good luck with that," I murmured. "Your Majesty."

V The Penultimate Chapter

In which are described the wondrous multitude of fabulous treasures and precious thyngs bestowed upon the kyng by his grayteful subjects in recognizance of his benevolent and magnanimous actyions undertaykne upon their behalf.

It must have been a slow news week, because the editor of the local paper, after seeing Dad's advertisement, decided to do a feature on the newest kingdom in its circulation area. It was either that or an article on potholes in supermarket car parks, and Dad's story won out.

I know that newspapers love wacky stories to fill their "Odd Spot" columns, but to my amazement, the story just grew and grew. Within a couple of days, the city paper had picked it up, then the radio, then the local TV station. Dad was in the social media newsfeeds. Suddenly, King Clive I's face was plastered all over the media. He was famous. And, as if to prove that there are more mad people out there than you think, he started getting fan mail.

WELCOME TO SUMMERDALE
Visitors with items
to declare,
take the red lane.
Visitors with nothing
to declare,
take the green lane.

The postie, who had read the papers and seen the TV, knew exactly where to deliver letters and parcels addressed to His Majesty, King Clive I, The Palace, Kingdom of Summerdale. Besides, Dad had erected a large sign over the driveway saying "Welcome to Summerdale. Visitors with items to declare, take the red lane. Visitors with nothing to declare, take the green lane."

Both lanes led to the front door, of course.

The postie went through the red lane and knocked on the door. "Letter for King Clive I," he chuckled, giving Dad a curtsey. "You know, technically, if you're a different country, these deliveries should have international stamps on them. But I'll let you off this time, Your Majesty."

That gave Dad an idea. "Stamps!" he said excitedly, rushing into the kitchen. "We'll issue our own stamps. They'll become collectors' items!" And it didn't stop there. Soon, he had me sitting in front of the computer designing stamps, coins, banknotes and flags. Dad printed out two copies of the flag and fixed them onto regal-looking coathangers twisted around the wing mirrors of his car.

"King Clive's Official Limousine," declared Dad.

"Shouldn't you break a bottle of champagne over its front bumper?" said Mum. "Didn't they launch the Titanic that way?" Luckily, Dad hadn't gotten around to building his dungeon yet. I figured he'd probably had difficulty ordering iron shackles and leather whips from the local hardware store.

Dad remembered the letter. It was from someone who, after explaining that he had $4300 in unpaid parking fines, was wondering if he could become a citizen of Summerdale to avoid going to court. Mum and I sighed. We knew what was going to happen next.

"Are you sure you want to do this?" queried the woman at the advertising desk at the local paper. She reread the piece of paper that Dad had handed over.

"The freedom of humanity from unfair tyranny demands it," replied Dad.

"I'll need a proper address," said the woman. "For the bill."

Dad summoned up all his majestic bearing, which mostly involved pulling in his tummy.

"That is a proper address, madam," said Dad.

"Can't you just pay by credit card like last time?" asked the woman wearily, resting her chin on her hand.

"OK," said Dad. He handed over his card. "Here's my foreign currency account."

"In a generous and chivalrous move, King Clive I extended the privileges enjoyed by his subjects to all and sundry from neighbouring countries, upon meeting the required criteria, which were published far and wide by foreign newspapers thus:

By order of King Clive I, honorary citizenship is hereby offered to persons of good character, or with $5.00, or both, who wish to swear allegiance to the rightful sovereign of Summerdale and enjoy the profound and generous benefits conferred upon them. We don't have any taxes, laws or no-watering days. Send your petitions for citizenship to the address below, with a stamped addressed envelope for reply."

A Humble and Fully Verified Eyewitness Account of the Ushering In of the Clivarian Era of Prosperity and Graciousness (Vol. V)

Applications from disgruntled victims of council watering inspectors, plumbing inspectors and clean air inspectors flooded in. I think even Dad was staggered by the response. He made $120 in the first week.

"You'd better design a citizenship certificate," he said, coming into my room. "And let's do some passports, too, because you never know when they might come in handy."

Things just snowballed. Dad issued a royal warrant vouching for the excellent products supplied by the local supermarket – "By Appointment to His Majesty King Clive I, Suppliers of Ice-Cream Cones, Toilet Paper and Sliced Bread." Mr Patel displayed it in his supermarket window, beneath the handwritten cards offering second-hand prams and trombones for sale. When the local paper did a story on that, and Mr Patel let slip that his sales of toilet paper had skyrocketed, suddenly every local business wanted a royal warrant – even the local takeaway store, whose poor hygiene standards had caused the outbreak of tummy bugs (and skyrocketing toilet paper sales) in the first place.

“By Appointment to His Majesty King Clive I, Suppliers of Chips, Fish and Battered Hot Dogs,” said its sign, after Dad had made Mr Kostopolous promise to wash his hands more often.

A tour bus rumbled down our street one day and a group of tourists stopped to take photographs of Dad shaking their hands. I know there’s not much to do in our city, but this was ridiculous. The Kingdom of Summerdale becoming a tourist attraction – who would have ever thought?

As often happens with kings, Dad was feeling invincible. He even moved the barbecue into the front yard, next to the red and green lanes, and took immense pleasure in turning innocent sausages into charcoal while flagrantly watering the rose bushes on Tuesdays. He should have read more history on the sites about monarchy he’d bookmarked on the internet. He’d have learned that just when kings start feeling invincible is usually the time they are surprised by being beheaded, deposed or tossed unceremoniously into their own dungeons. The inevitable happened.

VI The Final Chapter

In which occurs an account of the devious actyions employed by vyle curmudgeons and toady scalliwags, seeking to usurp the kyng's sovereign rights and powers, thus bringing much consternation to the kyng and his nobell court.

"Oi!" came a familiar voice from the darkness. "You can't do that!"

I was out the front, holding the hose while King Clive I was signing autographs. There always seemed to be curious onlookers lingering outside our gate now, or tour buses with bewildered Korean tour groups trying to reverse park between Mrs Willis's car and the official limousine. Dad made sure he waved benignly at everyone and gave autographs to those who wanted them. As he pointed out to Mum more times than were strictly necessary, he accepted the burden of his royal duties with grace and patience.

"Oi!" repeated the voice. "Have you got an RWE315?"

"Away with you, scoundrel!" said Dad with a dismissive wave of his hand. "This is a free country and I'll have you know that Princess Melanie has my blessing to use our rainwater on our state roses while I am attending to the needs of my people. You and your feeble pink slips have no authority here!"

"We'll see about that!" muttered the council watering inspector. Puffed up with the confidence that council directive 29F bestowed upon him, he marched towards our driveway, in no mood to argue with Dad.

"We're being invaded!" yelled Dad. "Release the royal hounds!"

"Are you sure?" I asked nervously. The council watering inspector looked like he meant business.

"Now!" commanded King Clive I. "Before he breaches our defences!"

I whistled. Valiant came trotting up the garden path and sniffed the council watering inspector's

trousers. Then he lifted his leg and, to the watering inspector's horror, proceeded to water the inspector's trousers.

"I'll have you for this!" spluttered the inspector indignantly.

"Royal personages do not demean themselves by speaking with knaves and vassals of foreign countries," said Dad. "You must address the ambassador to your country should you wish to enter into a dialogue with Summerdale."

"And who might that be?" demanded the enraged inspector.

"Mrs Willis, next door," said Dad.

Dad must have had an inkling that the council inspector was going to call the police because, while the inspector was next door, he raced inside and made a few phone calls of his own. By the time the police car arrived at the border of the Kingdom of Summerdale, reporters from the local paper,

NEWS

the city paper, the radio station and the local TV channel were gathered eagerly outside.

"I'm a prisoner of war!" cried Dad, as he was led to the back seat of the police car. "I'll be in touch with the United Nations about this!"

It must have been another really slow news day because King Clive I's arrest made the six o'clock news on TV and the front pages of all the papers in the morning. And the twitterverse went into overload.

The lawyer from Loopholes-R-Us peered over her glasses at Dad.

"It's the best deal I can get you," she said. "Take it or leave it."

Dad thought about his options. As a royal captive held at the mercy of a foreign land, he knew he didn't really have any.

"OK," he said. "But it'll have to happen in the Kingdom of Summerdale. I'm not going cap in hand – I mean, crown in hand – to some council office."

"I'll see what I can do," sighed the lawyer. "Now, you can get out of here if you pay your bail of $100. Have you got that much on you?"

"Do they take Kingdom of Summerdale dollars?" asked Dad hopefully. He fished around in his pocket. "Mel printed off a couple of million last week."

"Good luck with that," replied the lawyer.

The mayor, who was shrewd enough to see that King Clive I was getting even more coverage in the media than she was, pulled up outside the Kingdom of Summerdale. Dad, Mum and I were waiting to bestow our royal greetings upon her. With considerable foresight, we'd locked Valiant in the garden shed in case he was tempted to bestow his greetings upon her, too.

Cameras whirred and clicked as the mayor walked through passport control, and Dad held out his hand to her. They turned and faced the reporters and another barrage of clicks and flashes ensued.

"I hope you've got a resident parking sticker," Dad whispered to the mayor out the side of his mouth. "You need one around here, you know."

The diplomatic discussions that followed took three pots of tea and a packet and a half of chocolate biscuits to conclude. The mayor, who was aware that media coverage of her city had tripled since a fledgling kingdom had appeared in it, wanted to jump onto the bandwagon.

"It's good for tourism, too," she added, sipping her cup of tea. "Overseas visitors love to see royal pageantry. So, let's make a deal."

"Sounds OK to me," said Dad. "What kind of deal?"

"You let us use your 'kingdom' in our tourism promotions," said the mayor. "And we'll let you use our sewerage system, rubbish collection, postal service, electricity, telephone, water pipes, drainage, schools, hospitals, libraries and road network."

"We do have our own library," pointed out King Clive.

"CLIVE!" hissed Mum in a tone that was three octaves lower than her usual "Hmm".

"That's fine by me," said Dad hurriedly, with a weak smile at Mum.

"And there's the small matter of the fines," added the mayor.

"Don't I have diplomatic immunity?" said Dad.

"Don't push your luck," replied the mayor. "Deal or no deal?"

"And, with the signing of the peace treaty between the two glorious and neighbouring powers, a golden era of peace and prosperity descended upon the joyful citizens of both lands. The benevolent and popular King Clive I, in return for paltry tokens of gratitude from his neighbouring country, kindly allowed himself to eat cucumber sandwiches at the occasional council reception for tour group operators, and to bestow his royal wisdom upon distinguished guests at the city council and at children's parties.

At last, after the turbulent first year of nationhood, the Kingdom of Summerdale decided to hold a formal coronation for their blessed and selfless monarch. All who attended offered their sincere wishes for a long and happy reign."

A Humble and Fully Verified Eyewitness Account of the Ushering In of the Clivarian Era of Prosperity and Graciousness (Vol. VI)

And that, dear reader, is how it all really came about. That's the unofficial history of the Kingdom of Summerdale, but if you'd prefer to read the official version, all six volumes of *A Humble and Fully Verified Eyewitness Account of the Ushering In of the Clivarian Era of Prosperity and Graciousness* are available on our website for only $39.95 each (including postage and packing). Dad says all proceeds go to our foreign aid program. I think they go to paying off his fines.

Anyway, read them and then you can decide which version is more plausible. But don't tell King Clive I where you heard the unofficial version. The iron shackles and leather whips finally turned up from the hardware store and, as history so often shows, princesses have a nasty habit of being incarcerated in dungeons when they start telling tales.

I will, after all, be Her Most Glorious Majesty, Queen Melanie I, Defender of Liberty, Sovereign of Summerdale and Guardian of the Imperial Trident one day, and that just wouldn't do.